YO(

SLANG

A POCKET GUIDE TO YORKSHIRE WORDS & PHRASES

So you don't look stupid when trying to understand the Yorkshire accent

PREFACE

For people from outside of the region, the Yorkshire dialect can sound like a foreign language with an instantly recognisable accent. This mini illustrated 'dictionary' of Yorkshire words, sayings and explanations is here to rescue you.

AYE!

AHT

Out.

"We're going aht tonight for a drink."

ALLUS

Always.

"Allus wash your feet when they stink. That's all the time for you Nathan."

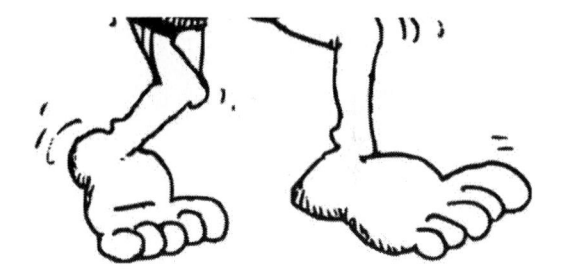

AM

I am.

"Am off t'bog."

AN ALL

As well.

"It was that cold the sheep were shivering an all."

ARSE

Used to describe a person behaving stupidly.

"You're such an arse at times Nathan."

ARSE END

The back end of something.

"Emma looks like the arse end of a donkey."

AYE

Yes.

"Emma said aye to a kiss behind the shed."

BABBI

Baby.

"Nathan stop crying like a babbi."

BACK END

The last bit.

"If we hurry we'll catch the back end of the film."

BACKY

Ride on the back of someone's bike.

"Give us a backy back to the house."

BAGSY

To claim something as yours.

"Bagsy the front seat of the car."

BAIRN

A child.

"The bairns are so cute when they play together."

BECK

A stream.

"Emma said she's off for a dip in't beck."

BELT

To hit.

"I'll belt you one in the face if you don't shut up Nathan."

BE REET

It will be ok.

"Don't worry about Emma, she'll be reet."

BERK

idiot.

"Nathan is a reet berk."

BOG

Toilet.

"Had far too many sausages for breakfast, I'm going t' bog."

BUTTY

Sandwich.

"I'll have brown sauce on that butty lass."

CACK HANDED

Left handed.
Clumsy.

"Nathan is very cack handed in the kitchen."

CHAMPION

Amazing.

"Last night's kebab was champion."

CHIP

Go.

"Let's chip Emma, it's boring here."

CHIPPY

Fish and chip shop.

"Can't wait for my chippy tea tonight."

CHUDDY

Chewing gum.

"Don't swallow your chuddy Nathan, it won't digest for 7 years."

CHUFFED

Happy. Pleased.

"Emma was chuffed with Nathan's results."

C'UNT

Could not.

"I c'unt see past Emma's behind."

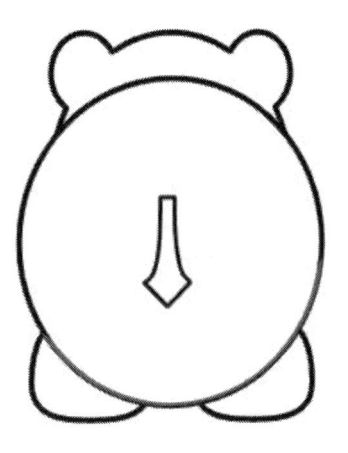

DALES

Yorkshire Dales.

"Nathan is off for a reet long walk in the Dales at weekend for some peace from Emma."

DEAD

Prefix for exaggeration or emphasis.

"That joke was dead funny. Unlike Nathan's face."

DID I 'ECKERS LIKE

No I did not.

"Did I 'eckers like eat the last Yorkshire pudding."

DOWN'T

Down to.

"Are you going down't Asda?"

DUNT

Don't.

"I dunt know why Nathan finds it so hard to understand Emma."

'EAD

Head (dropping the H at the beginning).

"Me 'ead 'urts after going t' pub."
"No Nathan, my 'ead 'urts listening to you going on about your 'ead 'urting."

'ECK

Heck (dropping the H at the beginning).
Hell.

"Flippin' 'eck, Emma's gorgeous."

EEE BY GUM

Oh my god.

"Eee by gum! Get that spider out of the house Nathan!"

EH

Pardon?

"Eh, what did you say?"

WH-WHAT?

EY UP

Hello.

"Ey up lad, 'ow are you?"

FAFFIN'

Fooling around.

"Stop faffin' around and get ready Nathan."

FLAGGIN'

Tired.

"Nathan was flaggin' by dinner time."

FRIGGIN'

Swear word.

"Oi Nathan you friggin' idiot, frig off."

GAFFER

The boss.

"Watch out, t' gaffer is on his way."
"We all know Emma is the gaffer in Yorkshire."

GAGGIN'

Thirsty, in need of a drink.

"I'm gaggin' for a pint."

GANDER

To have a look.

"Just went to the shops in York for a gander."

Gi'

Give.

"Gi' over and stop shouting Emma."

GINNEL

A small alleyway or snicket.

"Nathan took Emma down the ginnel but it was a dead end. that's why Emma didn't gi' over shouting at him."

GIP

Almost throw up.

"Your face is making me gip Nathan."

GIVE OVER

Behave.

"Give over Nathan, I don't want to touch your feet."

GIZ

Give me.

"Giz the remote Emma. Emmerdale is starting."

HACKY

Dirty.

"Emma was giving Nathan a hacky look when he got scared of the price."

'OW MUCH

A way of expressing something is too expensive.

"'Ow much!? In a bit."

ICE POP

An ice lolly.

"Nathan is fetching me an ice pop from the shop."

INABIT

Goodbye.

"I'm going to York for a night, inabit Emma."

IN'T

In the.

"Emma threw my phone in't bin when I got back from York."

JAMMY

Lucky.

"Nathan found a tenner the jammy bugger."

KEGS

Trousers

"Nathan you have a stain on your kegs. I'm not washing them for you again."

KEKS

Underwear.

"Nathan pure browned his keks last night. It went through to his kegs."

KIDDIN'

Joking.

"I'm only kiddin' Nathan, you don't have big ears."

LAD

Boy, man or son.

"How are you lad?"

LAMP

Punch or hit.

"Nathan I'll lamp you one if you don't get a move on."

LASS

Girl, wife or woman.

"Aye up to your lass from me."

LUG

Carry or pull.

"Just lug it over there in Nathan's room."

LUG 'OLE

Ear.

"Clean your lug 'oles Nathan because you never seem to hear me."

MANKY

Disgusting.

"Change your socks Nathan, they're manky."

MARDY

Bad mood or grumpy.

"Emma's being mardy today."

MIND

Be careful.

"Mind how you go, it's slippy out there."

MINGIN'

Disgusting.

"Nathan stop being so mingin' sitting there picking your nose."

MUTHA

Mother.

"Tell mutha I won't be home for dinner."

NAH THEN

Hello.

"Nah then young lad."

NAY

No. The opposite of yes.

*"Are you going down the pub tonight?"
"Nay, Emma said she wants me at home to watch Strictly together."*

NARKY

Moody.

"*Nathan was all narky about misplacing his phone whilst Strictly was on.*"

NOWT

Nothing.

"There's nowt left in the box."

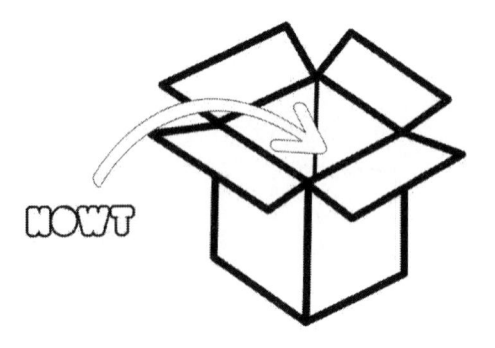

NOW THEN

Hello.

"Now then Nathan, what a fine day."

OH AYE

Really?

"Nathan was surprised when Emma asked him for his number."
"Oh aye."

'OW DO

How are you?

"'Ow do my love?"

OWT

Anything

"Are you doing owt tonight?"
"Aye, I have to stay in with Emma."

PAGGERED

Exhausted.

"I'm paggered staying in with Emma."

POP

Fizzy drink.

"Nathan fetch me some pop from the fridge."

PUT WOOD INT' HOLE

Close the door.

> "Thanks for the pop but how many times Nathan; Put wood int' hole. It is freezing!"

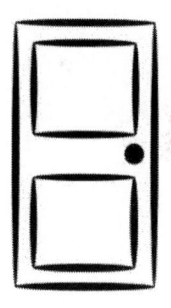

RADGED

Very angry.

"Emma was radged when she saw Nathan with another woman."

RANK

Disgusting.

"That smell is rank Nathan."

REEKS

Smells bad.

"Nathan your feet reek of rotten eggs."

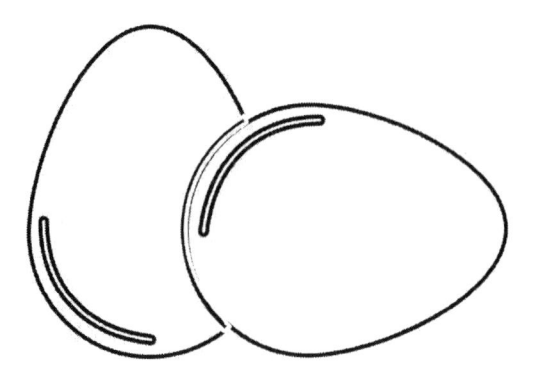

SCOLLOP

A slice of potato in batter deep fried.

"A scallop butty with ketchup please."

SCRAN

Food.

"I'm going out with Emma later for some scran."

SCRAPS

The loose bits of batter in your fish and chips.

"Save me some of your delicious scraps Emma."
"Get your own Nathan, you should've bought your scran."

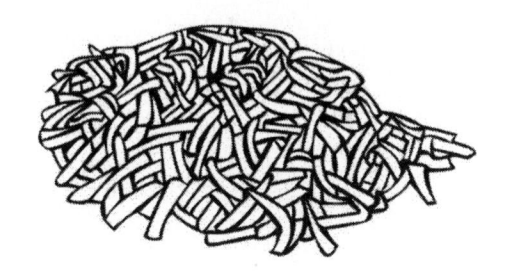

SHUT YA CAKEHOLE

Shut your mouth.

"You're talking nonsense Nathan, shut ya cakehole."

SNICKET

A small alleyway or ginnel.

"The cat ran into the snicket when it saw Emma."

SPROG

Child.

"Emma's pregnant with his sprog."

SPUD

Potato.

"Jacket spuds tonight with lots of butter...yum."

STROP

A tantrum or outburst.

"Nathan threw a strop when Emma asked for her dress back."

SUMMAT

Something.

"Ye got summat stuck in your teeth Nathan. And give back my dress."

T'

The.

"Am off t' pub tonight just for a couple."

TA

Thank you.

"Ta Emma for agreeing to let me go to the pub last night."

TARRA

Goodbye.

"Tarra Emma, see you tomorrow."

TEA CAKE

A bread roll (bap or bun).

"Gimme that tea cake, I'm hungry."

TEK

Take.

"Don't tek the mick out of my accent Nathan."

TIN TIN TIN

It isn't in the tin.

"I've checked and it tin tin tin."

T'WERK

Where Yorkshire people go 9-5 daily, to work.

"I can't stop, I'm off t'werk."

TWONK

An idiot.

"You're a twonk Nathan, do one."

WAZZOK

An idiot.

"Emma you're such a wazzok."

WHILE

Until.

"I'm working 6 while 8 tomorrow while you call me a Wazzok."

WI

With.

"What's up wi ya Nathan?"

WON'T FEEL BENEFIT

You will not feel the benefit of the temperature change.

"Take your coat off Nathan, you won't feel benefit when you go outside."

YEM

Home.

"I'm gannin yem because I couldn't feel the benefit."

YONDER

Over there.

"What's that I've spotted yonder?"
"Oh it's only Emma."

YORKSHIRE PUDDING

A pudding traditionally served with a Sunday roast.

"I can't wait for Sunday to taste Emma's delicious Yorkshire puddings."

YORKSHIRE TEA

The most popular tea sold in the UK, based in Harrogate.

"Put t' kettle on and have nice a cup of Yorkshire tea with me."

IN A BIT

IN A BIT

IN A BIT

IN A BIT

IN A BIT

IN A BIT

IN A BIT

IN A BIT

IN A BIT

IN A BIT

Printed in Great Britain
by Amazon